This book belongs to:

....

AUTUMN
PUBLISHING

Published in 2020
by Autumn Publishing
Cottage Farm
Sywell
NN6 0BJ
www.autumnpublishing.co.uk

0620 002
2 4 6 8 10 9 7 5 3
ISBN 978-1-83903-040-6

Illustrated by Lizzie Walkley
Written by Melanie Joyce

Cover designed by Nicholas Gage
Interiors designed by Alice Dainty
Edited by Jasmin Peppiatt

Printed and manufactured in China

I LOVE YOU
Grandad

AUTUMN PUBLISHING

I love you, Grandad,
you're a big cuddly bear.

You are so kind to me
and I know that you care.

You're the best **fun** a grandad could possibly be.

I love you so much...

... you mean everything to me.

"Let's explore!" you cry as we run out the door.

Our adventures are awesome.
I always want more.

I love you, Grandad,
because we giggle and play.

It's fun when you chase me
and I run away.

You never complain
when I make lots of noise...

... or eat secret treats...

... and don't tidy my toys.

You're so clever, Grandad, and wherever we go...

... you tell me lots of things that I didn't know.

Grandad,
I love you
because when my tears fall...

When I'm with you
I know there's **nothing** to fear.

You say so softly,

You are always safe here.

I snuggle up to you as the day turns to night.

We sit silently in the shimmering moonlight.

And when I fall asleep,
I know you won't be far.

I'll always love you because you're my Grandpa.